Mr. Louie Is Screwy!

Dan Gutman

Pictures by
Jim Paillot

SCHOLASTIC INC.

To Emma

ISBN 978-1-338-28511-6

12 11 10 9 8 7 6 5 4 3 2 1   18 19 20 21 22 23

Printed in the U.S.A.   40

First Scholastic printing, February 2018

Typography by Joel Tippie

Contents

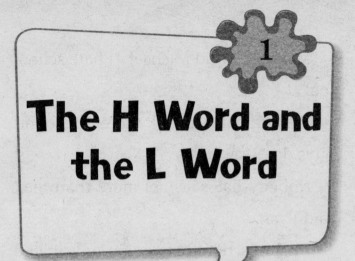

The H Word and the L Word

My name is A.J. and I hate school.

"I hate school," I told my friend Ryan, who will eat anything, even stuff that isn't food.

"Me too," he said. We were walking to Ella Mentry School with our friend Michael, who never ties his shoes.

"Me three," said Michael. "I hate school too."

"Well, I hate school more than you guys do," I said.

"Nobody hates school more than me," said Ryan.

"I hated school before you guys hated school," said Michael.

"Oh, yeah?" I told him. "I hated school before you were even born."

Any time you want to win an argument, just tell the other person you did something before they were born. It works every time. That's the first rule of being a kid.*

---

*This is called a footnote because when you see it, you're supposed to look down. To see your foot, you have to look down, too.

"Groovy!" somebody said as we were about to cross Walnut Street. "I can dig where you dudes are coming from."

It was Mr. Louie, our crossing guard! He was standing at the corner of Walnut Street in front of the school. Mr. Louie always wears sandals and a tie-dyed shirt. He held up his guitar, which he uses as a stop sign.

"But it's a drag to use the H word," Mr. Louie told us. "Hate is a downer, man. You should say 'love.'"

Ugh! Mr. Louie said the L word!

"Ewwww!" we all yelled.

"There's too much hate in the world," Mr. Louie explained, "and not enough love."

Mr. Louie used to be a judge, but he quit because he said there were too many bad vibes (whatever they are). That's when he became a crossing guard.

"The L word is for girls," I said.

"Love is for everyone," Mr. Louie told us. "Do you know why I *love* love so much? Every morning I take a love potion. You dudes should take some, too."

"No thanks!" we all said.

I never heard of a love potion. Maybe Mr. Louie was yanking our chain.

"School is cool," he said. "You dudes should say you love school."

"I'm not saying the L word out loud," I announced.

"A.J.," Mr. Louie told me, "if you don't say 'I love school,' I'm gonna tell everybody you love . . . Andrea!"

Ewwwwwwwwwwwwwwww!

Andrea Young is this really annoying girl in my class with curly brown hair. I don't love Andrea. I don't even like Andrea. I hate Andrea! So I sure didn't want Mr. Louie telling everybody I love her.

"Okay, okay," I said quietly, so nobody else would hear. "I love school."

"Outta sight!" said Mr. Louie. "Gimme some skin, A.J. Feel the love!"

"Oooooh!" Ryan said. "A.J. is in love with school!"

"When are you gonna get married to the school, A.J.?" asked Michael.

If those guys weren't my best friends, I would hate them.*

---

*What are you looking down here for? The story's up there, dumbhead!

I Hate Love

When we got to class, our teacher, Miss Daisy, was talking with Mr. Macky, the reading specialist. Reading is boring. But Mr. Macky loves reading so much, he walks around reading soup cans. He's weird.

"Do we have reading today?" I asked him.

"No," Mr. Macky told me, "we have an assembly."

An assembly is when everybody assembles in the all-purpose room. So it has the perfect name.

After the morning announcements, we had to walk a million hundred miles to the all-purpose room. It looked weird. There were peace signs, flowers, and lava lamps all over the stage.

"Crisscross applesauce," Miss Daisy told us as we sat down.

The teachers used to tell us to sit Indian style. But they stopped because they thought Indians might get mad. Then they told us to sit like pretzels. I guess some pretzels got mad, because now the teachers just say, "Crisscross applesauce." I hope applesauce doesn't get mad.*

Once everybody was seated, the strangest thing in the history of the world happened. Our principal, Mr. Klutz, got up onstage.

Well, that wasn't the strange part. Mr. Klutz gets up onstage all the time. The strange part was that he had hair all the way down to his shoulders!

We knew Mr. Klutz was wearing a wig, because just yesterday he was completely bald. Nobody can grow hair that fast. Mr. Klutz held up his hand and made a peace sign, which means shut up.

---

*Made you look down! Ha-ha! Man, you'll fall for anything!

"Valentine's Day is next week," Mr. Klutz told us, "so I invited a special guest. Put your hands together for . . ."

You'll never believe in a million hundred years who came out onstage.

It was Mr. Louie! Everybody clapped, because Mr. Louie is cool. I never saw him inside school before.

"Groovy!" said Mr. Louie. "I mean . . . like . . . you know?"

"Mr. Louie knows all about peace and love," Mr. Klutz told us, "so I asked him to help us celebrate Valentine's Day next week."

Mr. Louie played a song on his stop sign that was really easy to learn because

it went like this:

Love love love

Love love love

Love love love

That song had nothing but the L word

over and over again! It was dumb, but everybody clapped anyway, because we were glad it was over.

"Back in the Sixties," Mr. Louie told us, "everybody loved each other. Can you dig it? Don't you think the world would be a better place if everybody loved each other today?"

"Yes!" shouted all the girls.

"No!" shouted all the boys.

Mr. Louie said we were going to send cards, decorate the school with hearts and flowers, and have a big concert on Valentine's Day to celebrate peace and love.

"Let's show how much we love each other and make the world a hipper

12

place," he told us. "It's gonna be a gas. Love makes the world go round."

Ugh! I think Mr. Louie took too much of his love potion. All the boys were pretending to throw up.

Then Mr. Louie sang his favorite song, "If I Had a Hammer." It's about some weird guy who wants a hammer. If you ask me, instead of wasting time singing about wanting a hammer, he should just go to a hardware store and buy one.

After that Mr. Louie sang about some other weird guy who makes friends with ants.[*]

Finally the assembly was over. Miss

---

[*]It went like this: *"The ants are my friends, blowin' in the wind."*

Daisy made me the line leader. Andrea and her crybaby friend, Emily, were in line right behind me.

"Mr. Louie is right," Andrea told Emily. "Don't you *love* love? I *love* love. I *hate* hate."

She is so annoying. Anything Andrea says, I always say the opposite.

"I *hate* love," I said. "I *love* hate."

"Someday you're going to fall in love,

Arlo," said Andrea, who calls me by my real name because she knows I don't like it.

"Will not," I told her.

"Oh, yes you will, Arlo!" Andrea said. "You'll fall in love with some girl, and you'll comb your hair to look handsome for her."

"I don't think so," I said. "I never comb my hair."

"You'll get all goo-goo eyes over her, Arlo."

"No way."

"You'll hold hands with her, Arlo."

"Don't bet on it."

"You'll buy her valentines, Arlo."

"Fat chance."

"You'll kiss her, Arlo."

Ewww! Kissing? Disgusting! What is her problem? Why can't a truck full of valentines fall on Andrea's head?

Have Your Cake and Eat It, Too

3

A few days before Valentine's Day, we had to bring in valentines for the whole class. When I crossed Walnut Street with the guys, Mr. Louie held up his stop-sign guitar. He told us he was excited about the big Valentine's Day festival he was organizing.

"It's gonna be groovy," Mr. Louie said. "I'm lining up some big musical acts."

"Like who?" Ryan asked.

"Dig this," Mr. Louie said. "So far I've got Miss Holly, Mr. Docker, Mr. Loring, Ms. Hannah, Miss Small . . . "

"Those aren't musical acts," Michael said. "They're teachers!"

"We're gonna have a special surprise guest too," Mr. Louie said. But he wouldn't tell us who it was.

When we got to school, Miss Daisy and Mr. Macky were walking up the steps together. Miss Daisy was carrying a heart-shaped cake with bonbons on top. That's her favorite kind of candy.

"Do you have a special valentine, A.J.?" Mr. Macky asked me.

"No," I told him. "Valentines are dumb."

Actually, I did have a special valentine. My valentine is Mrs. Cooney, our school nurse. She is beautiful. Her eyes are like cotton candy. I would marry her when I grow up, but she's already married to some guy named Mr. Cooney. Bummer in the summer!

When we got to class, everybody wanted to eat cake. But Miss Daisy said we had to do writing first. I hate writing.

She told us to take out our valentine cards and a pencil. We had to write one thing we liked about every person in

the class.

I wrote Ryan's card first. It was easy:

I liked it when you ate the seat cushion on the school bus.

Then I wrote Michael's card:

I liked it when we watched the Super Bowl on your big-screen TV.

Then I wrote a card for Neil, who we call Neil the nude kid even though he wears clothes:

I liked it when you brought your ferret to school and it pooped on Emily's head.

It was harder to think of something I liked about the girls. This is what I wrote on Emily's card:

I liked it when that children's book author visited our school and her pet raptor attacked you.

I picked up Andrea's card. It was the hardest of all. I couldn't think of anything I liked about Andrea.

My mom always tells me that if you don't have anything nice to say about somebody, don't say anything at all. But I had to write *something* on Andrea's card. So I wrote this:

I liked it when you were absent on Take Our Daughters to Work Day.

Miss Daisy collected all the cards and sorted them while we did a math work sheet. Then she passed out all the valentines.

Emily looked at me. She was holding my card. Then she started crying and went running out of the room.

Sheesh, get a grip! What a crybaby! It wasn't my fault she got attacked by a raptor.

Andrea was reading my card too.

"That's horrible, Arlo!" she said.

"So is your face," I told her.

"You know, Arlo," Andrea said, "my mother says that when a boy acts mean to a girl, it means he's secretly in love with her."

"No it doesn't," I said. "It means he hates her."

"My mother is a psychologist," Andrea said. "She knows everything."

"Then she must know you're annoying," I told her.

Andrea thinks she's so smart. She was trying to get me to stop being mean to her by making me think I secretly like her. But I'm smart too. That's why I'm in the gifted and talented program.

Emily came back into the room. Miss Daisy made me apologize to her. I did, but I didn't mean it.

"What about you, Miss Daisy?" Andrea

asked. "Who's *your* valentine?"

"It's a secret," she replied.

"Ooooh, who is it?" we all asked.

"If I told you, it wouldn't be secret," Miss Daisy said.

"Please? Please? Please? Please? Please?"

Any time you want anything from a grown-up, just say Please over and over again. That's the first rule of being a kid. But Miss Daisy refused to tell us who her secret valentine was.

"Time for cake!" she announced.

Miss Daisy was totally trying to change the subject so we'd forget about her secret valentine. But I didn't care, because we were getting cake.

Emily passed out plates. Miss Daisy cut the cake. This girl named Annette put a piece on each plate.

"Psssst! A.J.!" Michael whispered. "I dare you to throw your cake at Andrea."

"Why don't you throw your cake at Andrea?" I whispered back.

"You're the one who hates her," Michael whispered. "You should throw your cake at her."

"I want to eat my cake," I whispered.

"A.J., if you don't throw your cake at Andrea," Michael whispered, "that means you love her."

"Yeah, A.J.," added Ryan. "It's true."

Annette put a piece of cake on my

plate. I was faced with the hardest decision of my life. Should I eat my cake, or should I throw it at Andrea?

If I ate it I would have yummy cake, but the guys would think I love Andrea. If I threw my cake at Andrea, the guys would know I hate her, and I would have the fun of seeing her get hit with cake. But I wouldn't get to eat it.

I couldn't decide what to do. I thought so hard that my brain hurt.

Finally I got the greatest idea in the history of the world! I broke my piece of cake in half. I ate one half and threw the other half at Andrea. It hit her right on the head!

Andrea turned around real fast.

"Who did that?" she shouted. "I know it was you, Arlo!"

I tried to whistle so it looked like I didn't throw the cake. Any time you don't want to be blamed for something, start whistling. That's the first rule of being a kid.

The only problem was that my mouth was full of cake. I couldn't whistle.

"It wasn't me," I said. "Hey, Andrea, do you like seafood?"

"Yes? Why?"

I opened my mouth.

"See?" I said. "Food!"

Andrea said I was gross. Then she rushed to the girls' room to clean the cake out of her hair.

One . . . two . . . three . . . four . . .

Do you know about the five-second rule? If you drop food on the floor and pick it up within five seconds, it's still okay to eat. That's because germs need at least six seconds to climb on the food.

When Andrea went to the bathroom, I rushed to pick the cake up off the floor. I got to it just before five seconds were up. Then I ate it.

I had my cake and ate it, too! Nah-nah-nah boo-boo on Andrea!

It was the greatest day of my life.

The Power of Love

The next morning me and a bunch of other kids were waiting at the corner to cross Walnut Street.

"It's almost Valentine's Day," Mr. Louie told us as he held up his stop-sign guitar. "That's when love is the most powerful. Are you kids feeling the power of love?"

"Yes!" said all the girls.

"No!" said all the boys.

"Love is so strong," Mr. Louie told us, "I'll bet we can use our love to levitate the school!"

"'Levitate'?" somebody asked. "What's that?"

I knew that word. "Levitate" means to make something float up in the air. I'm in the gifted and talented program, so I know big words like that. Besides, I saw it in a comic book once. This magician was levitating a lady. Then he cut her in half with a saw. It was cool.

"We can't make the school float up in the air," I said.

"Sure we can," Mr. Louie insisted. "You kids can accomplish anything if you put your minds to it. So let's put our minds to it. Close your eyes and focus the awesome power of your love."

I had to admit that it would be cool to make the school levitate. Maybe if we tried really hard, we could make it float away. Then we wouldn't have to go to school anymore.

We all closed our eyes and tried to levitate the school.

"Is it floating?" Ryan asked.

"Not yet," Mr. Louie said. "We need more love!"

I concentrated really hard and tried to

levitate the school. Then I opened my eyes. The school was still sitting there on the ground, just like it always is.

"It's not working," Michael said. "Levitating a school is impossible."

"You gotta keep your eyes closed," Mr.

Louie told us. "Try one more time. Close your eyes real tight and concentrate. Use the power of your love!

"Love . . . love . . . love . . . love . . ."

I closed my eyes and concentrated so hard that my brain hurt.

A few seconds went by. Then Mr. Louie suddenly shouted, "You did it! Right on!"

I opened my eyes. The school was just sitting there on the ground.

"It's not levitating," Ryan said.

"It was when your eyes were closed," Mr. Louie said. "I saw it! Outta sight! The school was floating two feet off the ground! You kids are awesome. Man, love is powerful!"

I'm not sure if we really levitated the
school or if he was just yanking our
chain. But I do know one thing for sure.

Mr. Louie is screwy!

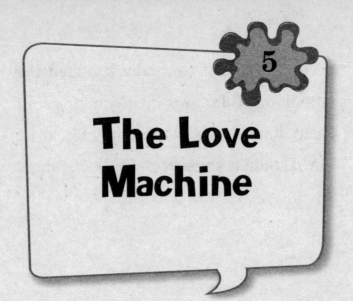

The Love Machine

I don't know if the school was really floating, but the L word was definitely in the air the day before Valentine's Day. In art class, Ms. Hannah had us cut big hearts out of red paper to put all over the hallways. In music class, Mr. Loring had us sing love songs. The lunch lady,

Ms. LaGrange, made us heart-shaped Tater Tots.

In the library, Mrs. Roopy dressed up like Cupid and read us a book about Valentine's Day in other countries. Did you know that in Slovenia birds get married to each other? And in Korea on April 14 men who didn't get a present on Valentine's Day gather together and eat noodles.

Other countries are weird.

That afternoon we had computer class with Mrs. Yonkers, who is a genius. One time she invented a computer that turned vegetables into junk food. She should get the No Bell Prize. That's a prize they give to people who don't have bells.

Mrs. Yonkers told us that she worked all weekend on a new invention called the Love Machine.

"What does it do?" Andrea asked.

"It reads brain waves," Mrs. Yonkers said, "and it shows what you love and what you hate."

We all wanted to try the Love Machine. Michael got to go first, because he was sitting with his hands folded. Mrs. Yonkers attached some wires to his head and turned on the Love Machine.

"I . . . LOVE . . . FOOTBALL!" said a computery voice. "I HATE . . . GOING TO THE DENTIST."

Wow! The Love Machine really worked! Michael does love football, and I know he hates going to the dentist. Mrs. Yonkers took the wires off Michael's head and attached them to Ryan's head.

"I HATE . . . GETTING SHOTS," the voice said. "I . . . LOVE . . . BROCCOLI."

Wow! Ryan really does love broccoli. He's weird.

Andrea got to go next. Mrs. Yonkers

hooked the wires up to her head.

"I HATE . . . MEAN PEOPLE," said the voice. "I . . . LOVE . . . SCHOOL." What a sick, twisted mind Andrea has!

Mrs. Yonkers called on me next. She stuck the wires to my head. They felt cold.

"We know what A.J. loves," Ryan said. "Skateboarding . . . video games . . . dirt bikes . . . football . . ."

"I HATE . . . SCHOOL," the voice suddenly said. "I . . . LOVE . . . ANDREA."

WHAT???????????????????

"Oooooh!" everybody went.

"That thing is busted!" I told Mrs. Yonkers. "I want a do over!"

Mrs. Yonkers said she had to give everybody else a chance first. The whole class started singing that song about me and Andrea sitting in a tree, K-I-S-S-I-N-G.

I thought I was gonna die. It was the worst day of my life.

There was only one thing I could do— run away to Antarctica and live with the penguins. Penguins are cool, and they wouldn't care that the dumb Love Machine said I loved Andrea.

Klutzstock

My mother wouldn't drive me to Antarctica to live with the penguins.

"Why not?" I asked.

"Because I don't want to miss the big love festival!" she said. "All the other parents are going to be there!"

It was the worst day of the year—

Valentine's Day. The L day! And to make things even worse, I had to go to school with my mom.

When we got to the field behind Ella Mentry School, there was a big sign across the soccer goal: WELCOME TO KLUTZSTOCK! A stage was set up with speakers on each side.

Parents, teachers, and kids were spreading out blankets on the grass. Some of them were dressed like hippies. Everybody was making peace signs and saying stuff like "Groovy!" and "Far-out!"

Andrea and Emily saw me and came over. They were wearing tie-dyed shirts, sandals, headbands, and flowers in their hair.

"Isn't this groovy, Arlo?" said Andrea. "We're flower children."

"Far-out!" Emily said.

Ugh! They were even more annoying than usual. I got away from them and walked around until I spotted Michael, Ryan, and Neil the nude kid.

"Who do you think the surprise guest is gonna be?" Neil asked.

"I bet it'll be our old music teacher, Mr.

Hynde," Ryan said. "Remember when he came back to school and—"

Ryan didn't get the chance to finish his sentence, because Mr. Louie got up onstage and started talking into the microphone.

"Walnut Street is closed, man!" he said. "Far-out!"

"Far-out!" everybody yelled.

"Happy Valentine's Day," Mr. Louie said. "We're here to groove on three hours of peace and music. So kick back and dig the vibes. If you get thirsty, be sure to use the water fountain next to the stage."

The first act was Mr. Klutz. He played

"The Star-Spangled Banner" on a kazoo.

Everybody clapped.

Miss Holly, the Spanish teacher, came out with a basket of fruit on her head. She sang a love song in Spanish.

Miss Patty, the school secretary, played an accordion.

Ms. Coco, the gifted and talented teacher, read a love poem while Ms. Hannah played a bongo drum.

A bunch of the other teachers got up and sang. Mostly they were terrible. But everybody in the crowd clapped anyway. We didn't want to hurt their feelings. Between songs, me and the guys kept going to the water fountain to get drinks.

"And now it's time for our special surprise guest," announced Mr. Louie. "Put your hands together for my favorite rock-and-roll band of all time . . . KISS!"

Everybody went crazy when four guys in big boots and weird makeup got up on stage with guitars.

"Far-out!" somebody in the crowd yelled.

Then we realized it wasn't the *real* Kiss. It was our librarian, Mrs. Roopy; the bus driver, Mrs. Kormel; our science teacher, Mr. Docker; and our gym teacher, Miss Small. They were all dressed up like Kiss.

Then they started playing—really loud! Mrs. Roopy was the lead singer.

"I . . . *wanna read and write all night, and check out books all day,*" she sang. "*I . . . wanna read and write all night, and check out books all day . . .*"

Everybody got up and started dancing. Mr. Klutz was dancing with Miss Lazar. Mr. Loring was dancing with Ms. Coco. Mr. Macky was dancing with Miss Daisy. Onstage, Mrs. Roopy stuck out her tongue. Flames started shooting out of her guitar. Smoke started coming out of the floor. It was cool.

We were really hot from all that dancing, so me and the guys went to the water fountain again. Mr. Louie was there, moving around with his eyes closed.

"Klutzstock is outta sight!" he said. "Are you dudes grooving on the vibes?"

"Oh, yeah," Ryan said, "it's far-out."

"When do we vote?" I asked Mr. Louie.

"Vote?" he asked. "Vote for what?"

"Vote to see who gets kicked out," I told him.

"Oh, no, that's not my bag," Mr. Louie said.

"You mean nobody gets eliminated, like on a reality TV show?" asked Michael.

"No, man. This is all about the love," Mr. Louie said. "There are no winners or losers. Just good vibrations."

"Aren't you going to have judges insult the singers and make them cry?" asked Ryan.

"No! Dig the tunes, man," Mr. Louie said. "Groove to the beat."

Mr. Louie could tell I was disappointed that none of the teachers would be humiliated. He put his arm around my shoulder.

"Let me clue you in on a little secret, A.J.," he told me. "I spiked the water fountain."

"What do you mean?" I asked.

"Shhhh! I put something in the water," Mr. Louie whispered.

"What'd you put in the water?" I asked.

"Remember I told you about my love potion?" he said. "Well, you've been drinking it. Do you feel the love yet? Happy Valentine's Day!"

AHHHHHHHHHHHHHHHHHHHHH!

Kissing Is Gross

As soon as Mr. Louie told us he put love potion in the water fountain, me and the guys spit out the water. Ugh! Disgusting!

"There's love potion in there?" I asked.

"Right on," Mr. Louie said. "Love is the most powerful force in the universe. It helped you levitate the school."

Mrs. Roopy and her band finished their song. Andrea, Emily, and Annette came over to drink from the water fountain.

"Isn't this fab, Arlo?" asked Andrea.

"It's a heavy scene, man," Emily said.

Annette nodded. "Totally."

Just then a weird feeling came over me. I didn't know what it was, but suddenly I had this urge to give Andrea a kiss!

So I did! I kissed her.

Ahhhhhhhhhhhhhhhhhhhhhhh!

"Why, Arlo," Andrea said, all smiley. "How sweet! I didn't know you liked me."

"I don't!" I yelled. "It's the water! Mr. Louie put love potion in it!"

"He did?" Andrea, Emily, and Annette asked at the same time.

You'll never believe in a million hundred years what happened next.

Emily kissed Ryan!

Then Michael kissed Annette!

Word must have spread through the crowd that Mr. Louie put love potion in the water fountain. Because the next

thing we knew, teachers started kissing each other! Parents started kissing each other! Everybody was kissing each other!

Gross! This was the worst Valentine's Day in the history of the world!

Teachers in Love

8

For the rest of my life, I would have to live with the fact that I kissed Andrea. But I had to be a man about it.

The next morning Andrea and Emily and the other girls were all whispery and giggly. Miss Daisy hadn't come in yet. I put my backpack away and marched over to Andrea.

"I just want you to know that I still hate you," I told her. "I only kissed you because I drank that love potion Mr. Louie put in the water fountain."

"I know," Andrea said. "I hate you too, Arlo."

"Good," I said. "As long as we're in agreement."

"But guess what, Arlo?"

"Your butt?" I replied.

Any time anyone says, "Guess what?" you should always answer, "Your butt." That's the first rule of being a kid.

"Miss Daisy has a boyfriend!" she said, all excited.

"What? No way!"

"She does!" said Emily.

"Who is it?" I asked.

"It's Mr. Macky!" Andrea said, and all the girls collapsed in giggles.

Michael, Ryan, and some of the boys came over.

"Miss Daisy and Mr. Macky?" Ryan asked. "Girlfriend and boyfriend? Impossible!"

"How do you know?" I asked Andrea.

"Haven't you noticed they've been hanging around each other lately?" Andrea asked. "And sometimes they walk to school together."

"Mr. Macky is always coming into our class," said Annette, "even when we don't have reading."

"I saw them making goo-goo eyes at each other at Klutzstock," Emily said. "They're in love!"

"And this morning," Andrea whispered, "I walked by the Reading Recovery Room and I saw them holding hands!"

The Reading Recovery Room is Mr. Macky's office. The girls collapsed in giggles again.

"Maybe they were just shaking hands," I said.

"They weren't shaking, Arlo," Andrea said. "They were holding."

"Maybe Mr. Macky was putting her under arrest," I suggested. "He held her hand so she couldn't escape."

"He wasn't arresting her, Arlo," Andrea insisted.

"Maybe they were arm wrestling?" I guessed.

"They weren't arm wrestling, Arlo," said

Andrea. "They're in love!"

Ewwww! Disgusting!

"Maybe they're gonna get married!" Emily said.

"They can't get married," said Neil the nude kid. "They're teachers."

"If Miss Daisy marries Mr. Macky, she'll be Mrs. Macky," Annette said.

"Maybe she'll keep her name," said Andrea. "Lots of women do that. Then she'll be Mrs. Daisy."

"Maybe she'll combine their two names," Ryan suggested. "She could be Mrs. Dacky or Mrs. Maisy."

All the girls were giggling and gossiping about what Miss Daisy would wear to her wedding and where she and Mr. Macky would go on their honeymoon.

"There isn't going to be a honeymoon!" I shouted. "They're not going out!"

"Who's not going out?" somebody behind us asked.

It was Miss Daisy!

Everybody stopped talking.

"Where were you, Miss Daisy?" asked Ryan.

"I was in the Reading Recovery Room," Miss Daisy said.

"Um-hmmmmm," Andrea said, looking at me.

"Is Mr. Macky your boyfriend?" demanded Michael.

"Oh, I don't know!" Miss Daisy giggled. But her face turned red like a tomato. That's a sure sign that somebody has something to hide. "You'll have to ask—"

She didn't get the chance to finish her sentence, because guess who walked into the door at that very moment?

Nobody, because walking into a door would hurt. But guess who walked into the door*way*.

It was Mr. Macky!

"Is Miss Daisy your girlfriend?" we all asked.

Mr. Macky didn't say a word. Instead, he leaned over and kissed Miss Daisy!

Ewwww! Disgusting! They were

smooching! Call the nurse! I thought I
was gonna throw up.

"Oooooh!" Ryan said. "Miss Daisy and
Mr. Macky are in love!"

"When are you gonna get married?"
asked Michael.

"Next Sunday," replied Miss Daisy.

WHAT?????????!!!!!!!!!!!!!!

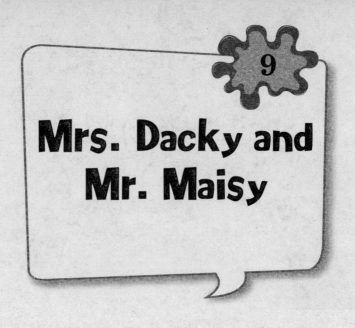

Mrs. Dacky and Mr. Maisy

It had to be a joke. Miss Daisy and Mr. Macky couldn't be getting married!

But it was true. Miss Daisy told us that Mr. Macky had been her boyfriend for a long time, but they kept it secret. Then, at Klutzstock, he got down on one knee and proposed to her.

Miss Daisy showed us her engagement ring.

"It's beautiful!" said all the girls.

Miss Daisy and Mr. Macky were going to get married on Sunday, and our whole class was invited to the wedding! Mr. Louie, who used to be a judge, was going to marry them in a church.

Well, the girls got all super-girly—even girlier than usual. They were all hugging Miss Daisy and giggling and crying and saying how happy they were.

"Is your new name going to be Mrs. Macky?" asked Andrea.

"How about Mrs. Dacky or Mrs. Maisy?" asked Ryan.

"Gee, I don't know," said Miss Daisy, who doesn't know anything. "Maybe I'll hyphenate my name."

"Once they had to hyphenate me at a Pee Wee football game," I said. "I almost passed out. But then they gave me something to drink and I was okay."

"That's 'hydrate,' dumbhead," Andrea told me. "'Hyphenate' means to put a dash between two words."

"I knew that," I lied.

Mr. Macky and Miss Daisy were all lovey-dovey, making goo-goo eyes at each other. The girls started planning the wedding. They were talking about what they were going to wear, what presents they should bring, and who Miss Daisy and Mr. Macky's children would look like.

I pulled the guys over to the other side of the room. We huddled like a football team.

"This is horrible," I told them. "This is the worst day in the history of the world."

"What's the big deal, A.J.?" asked Michael. "People get married all the time."

"Yeah, but Mr. Macky and Miss Daisy aren't in love," I told him. "He only asked her to marry him because of the love potion Mr. Louie put in the water fountain."

"I think it's nice that Miss Daisy is going to get married," said Neil the nude kid.

"Don't you get it?" I told Neil. "Miss Daisy is the perfect teacher. She can't read, write, or do math. But if she gets married, she might have a baby and quit working. Then we'll get a real teacher!"

"A.J.'s right!" Ryan said. "A real teacher will force us to learn stuff."

"That would be horrible!" agreed Michael.

"So what can we do about it?" asked Neil.

There was only one thing to do.

"We have to stop the wedding," I told them.

Sabotage!

Did you ever hear the word "sabotage"? It's a great word. "Sabotage" is a fancy way to say "mess stuff up." I'm really good at messing stuff up.

I learned about sabotage from a spy movie. These good guys blew up a truck to sabotage some bad guys. It was cool.*

---

*There hasn't been a footnote in a long time, has there?

But how do you sabotage a wedding? Blowing up a truck would probably not be a good idea.

"Maybe we can leave a trail of bonbons leading away from the church," suggested Ryan. "Then Miss Daisy will follow the trail and miss her own wedding."

"She's dumb," Michael said, "but she's not that dumb."

"We have to convince her that she shouldn't marry Mr. Macky," I told the guys.

"How can we do that?" asked Neil the nude kid. "Andrea and the other girls will mess everything up."

Neil was right. If we tried to convince

Miss Daisy not to marry Mr. Macky, the girls were sure to sabotage our plan.

But then I remembered something. In the morning, all the girls were going to the nurse's office to be weighed and measured with Mrs. Cooney. It would be our big chance!

The next morning I waited until the girls left before telling Miss Daisy we had a wedding present for her.

"I love presents!" she said.

I went to my cubby and got out my old skateboard. I had put a ribbon around it to make it look better.

"There's gum in the wheels so they don't spin very fast anymore," I told her.

"But we wanted you to have it."

"Oh, thank you, A.J.!" Miss Daisy said as she gave me a hug. "That is so thoughtful!"

"We're really happy that you and Mr. Macky are getting married," I lied.

"Yeah, we think it's great," said Ryan.

"I'm glad to hear you boys say that," Miss Daisy said.

"It's nice that you fell in love with Mr. Macky," I told her, "even though he's . . . uh . . . different."

"Different?" Miss Daisy asked. "What's different about him?"

"Well, did you know that Mr. Macky has six toes?" I asked her.

"Really? I didn't know that," said Miss Daisy, who doesn't know anything.

"Yup, six toes on each foot," I said.

"And they're webbed," added Michael. "Like a duck."

"Well, nobody's perfect," Miss Daisy said.

Hmmmm. It didn't seem to bother Miss Daisy that she

was marrying a guy with webbed feet. I would have to try something else.

"You know, I was in the post office yesterday with my mom," I told her, "and guess whose picture was on the wall? Mr. Macky's!"

"Is that so?" said Miss Daisy.

"Yeah," I told her. "Did you know he robbed a bank in Texas?"

"I didn't know that," Miss Daisy said.

"I hear he's wanted for a string of armed robberies in Oklahoma, too," said Neil the nude kid.

"Oh, dear!" exclaimed Miss Daisy.

"He's not even a real reading teacher," Michael said. "He kidnapped our reading teacher and is holding him for ransom. That happens all the time, y'know."

"My word!" said Miss Daisy.

"I heard that he snores, too," I mentioned. "It's like sleeping in the same room with a moose."

"Hmmmmm," said Miss Daisy.

It was working like a charm! You could tell Miss Daisy was thinking things over. Maybe she would change her mind about marrying Mr. Macky.

Speaking of which, guess who came in at that very moment? Mr. Macky! He kissed Miss Daisy and told her she could hang out in the Reading Recovery Room while he did a lesson with us.

Perfect! Now we could work on him.

"We wanted to tell you how happy we are for you and Miss Daisy," I told Mr. Macky.

"Yeah, we think it's great that you're getting married," said Ryan.

"I'm glad I have your support, boys," Mr. Macky said. "Let's open our reading books to page twenty-three."

"Yeah, it's nice that you fell in love with

Miss Daisy," I told him, "even though she's . . . uh . . . different."

"What's different about her?" he asked.

"Well, for one thing, she's addicted to bonbons," I told him.

"So am I!" said Mr. Macky. "Miss Daisy and I have a lot in common. Let's turn to page twenty-three."

"Do you eat your own boogers, too?" asked Ryan. "That's what Miss Daisy does."

"Really?" said Mr. Macky. "That's great! If she eats her own boogers, we won't have to do much grocery shopping! Page twenty-three, please."

"She doesn't eat her own boogers,"

Michael said. "She blows her nose into the garbage can!"

"Terrific!" said Mr. Macky. "We'll save money on tissues. Let's turn to page twenty-three."

Mr. Macky is wacky!

"Did you know that Miss Daisy likes burning ants with a magnifying glass for the fun of it?" asked Neil the nude kid.

"Yes!" Mr. Macky replied. "That's what we did on our first date. Page twenty-three."

Our sabotage plan was totally not working with Mr. Macky. It was time to use the one weapon that I knew would work for sure. Mr. Macky is a reading teacher. He loves reading more than anything else.

"Did you know that Miss Daisy doesn't know how to read?" I asked. "Do you really want to marry a dumbhead?"

"Yes!" Mr. Macky said. "That's why I asked her to marry me. I've been searching for years to find a woman who would let me read to her."

I slapped my forehead. It was useless! There was no way to convince Mr. Macky not to marry Miss Daisy.

Miss Daisy came back to class and Mr. Macky whispered something in her ear.

"We're glad you boys are concerned about us," Mr. Macky said, "but Miss Daisy and I are in love. We hope we'll see you at the church on Sunday."

Then they started smooching again. Ugh! Disgusting!

We were all depressed. On the way home, we told Mr. Louie that our plan to sabotage the wedding failed.

"You can't stop love," Mr. Louie said. "It's like I told you, dudes. Love is stronger than hate. Love is the most powerful thing in the world."

That's when I got a genius idea. In fact,

I got two genius ideas!

But I'm not going to tell you what they are.

Okay, okay, I'll tell you. But you have to read the next chapter. So nah-nah-nah boo-boo on you.

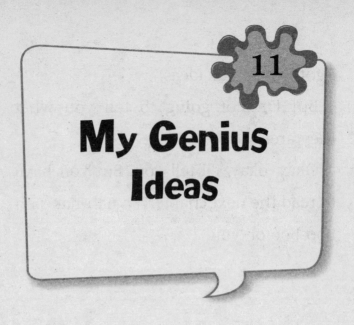

My Genius
Ideas

11

Okay, here's genius idea #1: Me and the guys would hold a protest rally in front of the church and stop the wedding.

Mr. Louie had told us that back in the Sixties, kids were always protesting stuff. He said if you didn't like something, you could protest and change the world. I didn't like Miss Daisy getting married, so the best way to stop it would be to protest.

On the morning of the wedding, my mom said I had to wear a jacket and tie. What's up with that? Why do men have to wear a dumb cloth around their neck? Whoever thought up that idea should get the Nobrain Prize. That's a prize they give to people who don't have brains.

I went to the church with my parents. Michael, Ryan, and Neil the nude kid were waiting out front. I told my parents to go inside and I would meet them in there.

"Okay, let's do this!" I told the guys.

The four of us formed a line and

started marching back and forth in front of the church.

"DOWN WITH LOVE!" I chanted. "LOVE STINKS!"

"NO MORE KISSING!" Ryan chanted. "KISSING SPREADS GERMS!"

"STOP THE WEDDING!" Michael chanted.

"GIRLS HAVE COOTIES!" chanted Neil the nude kid.

We were hoping other boys would join our protest, but nobody did. It was just the four of us marching back and forth. That's when Mr. Louie came out of the church. He was wearing a black robe.

"What up, dudes?" he asked.

"We're protesting against the wedding," I told him. "You said if somebody doesn't like something, they should protest."

"Protesting against love is a bummer," Mr. Louie told us. "Come inside and sit down."

So much for genius idea #1. It was time to try genius idea #2.

Me and the guys went in the church and sat down together.* I had been to one wedding before. It was at our school, when Mr. Klutz married a pig. But I don't think that was a real wedding, because Mr. Klutz was already married to a human being named Mrs. Klutz.

Mr. Louie stood at the front of the church. All our teachers were there. Mr. Klutz brought his wife (who wasn't a pig). Mrs. Cooney was there with some guy named Mr. Cooney. I hate him.

---

*Do you know why it smells in church? Because you have to sit in your own pew.

"Is it time?" Ryan whispered to me.

"Not yet."

My tie was choking me and I was really thirsty. But there was no way I was gonna drink from the water fountain. Mr. Louie probably put his love potion in that one too.

There was no time to get a drink anyway, because some lady started playing that "Here Comes the Bride" song on the organ. Miss Daisy came from the back of the church and walked down the aisle with some old guy. She looked really pretty in her wedding dress.

Then Mr. Macky walked across the aisle and stood next to Miss Daisy.

"Is it time?" Michael whispered.

"Almost."

"Dearly beloved," Mr. Louie announced, "we are gathered here together to join this groovy couple in holy matrimony."

It was time.

"Okay, now!" I whispered to the guys.

This was my genius idea: we were

going to levitate Mr. Louie. If we could make him float up in the air and out of the church, he wouldn't be able to perform the wedding ceremony. Me, Ryan, Michael, and Neil the nude kid all closed our eyes and tried to levitate Mr. Louie.

"It's not working!" Ryan said.

"Close your eyes!" I told him. "It doesn't work unless your eyes are closed!"

This was a problem. With my eyes closed, I couldn't tell if Mr. Louie was levitating. And I couldn't levitate him with my eyes open.

"Is he floating?" asked Michael.

"I don't think so," Neil said.

"We need more love!" I told them.

We kept trying to levitate Mr. Louie for a long time. I concentrated so hard that my brain hurt. When I opened my eyes, Mr. Louie wasn't at the front of the church anymore. Maybe it had worked. Maybe he had floated away!

But then I saw him. He was coming over to us!

"Dudes," he said, "what are you doing?"

I didn't know what to say. I didn't know what to do. I had to think fast.

"Uh, we're just grooving on the love vibes," I told him.

"I can dig that," Mr. Louie said. "Gimme some skin."

We all slapped Mr. Louie's hand, and he

returned to the front of the church to continue the ceremony.

"That levitation thing didn't work at all," Ryan whispered in my ear. "Do you have any other genius ideas?"

"No, I'm out."

Oh, well. We tried our best. There was nothing I could do now. It was out of my hands. Mr. Louie said a bunch of lovey-dovey stuff about Mr. Macky and Miss Daisy. He told everyone how they met in the teachers' lounge and fell in love.

"Do you, Mr. Macky, take this woman to be your lawfully wedded wife?" Mr. Louie asked.

"I do."

"Do you, Miss Daisy, take this man to be your lawfully wedded husband?"

"I do."

"Is there anybody here who knows why these lovebirds should not be united in wedded grooviness?" asked Mr. Louie. "Speak now or forever hold your peace."

I looked at Michael. Michael looked at Ryan. Ryan looked at Neil. Then they all looked at me. You could hear a pin drop.

"Stop the wedding!" I shouted, standing up.

Now everybody in the church was looking at me.

"A.J.!" shouted my mother.

"Mr. Macky and Miss Daisy are not in

love!" I yelled. "They just think they are.
He only asked her to marry him because
Mr. Louie put love potion in the water
fountain at school!"

Everybody gasped.

"That's the craziest thing I ever heard," said Mr. Klutz. "Is this true?"

"I was just jiving you, A.J.," Mr. Louie said. "There's no such thing as love potion."

"There isn't?" I asked. "What about levitating the school? Were you jiving about that too?"

"Yeah, I was just yanking your chain, A.J. Don't flip your wig."

I sat down.

This was terrible! Do you realize what this means? If there was no love potion in the water, it means I kissed Andrea . . . because I *wanted* to! It means the Love

Machine must have been right when it said I loved Andrea!

I love Andrea!

Ewwwwww! Disgusting!

I thought I was gonna die. Now I would really have to run away to Antarctica and live with the penguins.

"I now pronounce you husband and wife," Mr. Louie said. "Dude, you may kiss the bride."

Mr. Macky and Miss Daisy kissed. It was gross, but nice, too. It was a real Kodak moment.

Happily Ever After

As soon as the wedding was over, I took off my dumb tie and ran to the water fountain. I really needed to get hyphenated.

Mr. Klutz was handing out bags of rice, and he told us to throw the rice when Mr. Macky and Miss Daisy came out of the church. Cool!

"Rice fight!" I yelled.

Me, Michael, Ryan, and Neil ran around throwing rice at everybody. I nailed Andrea in the face. I threw some rice at that Mr. Cooney guy, too. Serves him right for marrying Mrs. Cooney.

It was cool. You should have been there! We kept throwing rice until Mr. Louie told us to knock it off.

Mr. Macky and Miss Daisy got into a car. There were a bunch of cans tied to the bumper with string. What's up with that? People who tie cans to their car are weird.

Finally, Mr. Macky and Miss Daisy drove away. We all waved good-bye as the cans rattled down the street.

I guess we won't see Miss Daisy or Mr. Macky for a while. Maybe Mr. Klutz will forget to hire a new teacher and we can just have fun all day. Or maybe we'll get a teacher who's even dumber than Miss Daisy.

Maybe Mr. Macky and Miss Daisy will

get divorced and everything will be back to normal. Maybe Mrs. Cooney will divorce her husband and

marry me instead. Maybe Mr. Louie will realize that the Sixties are over. Maybe Mr. Klutz will grow some real hair so he won't have to wear a silly wig. Maybe an elephant will fall on Andrea's head and nobody will find out that I love her.

Maybe I'll figure out how to levitate stuff. That would be cool.

But it won't be easy!

Dan Gutman

has written many weird books for kids. He lives with his weird wife in New York (a very weird place).

Jim Paillot

lives in Arizona (another weird place) with his weird wife and two weird children. Isn't that weird?